Every
Thing
On
It

Every Thing On It

poems and drawings by

Shel Silverstein

HARPER
An Imprint of HarperCollinsPublishers

Every Thing On It

© 2011 Evil Eye, LLC.

The Shel Silverstein name and signature logo are trademarks of Evil Eye, LLC.

Library of Congress Cataloging-in-Publication Data is available.

Library of Congress Control Number: 2011924606

ISBN 978-0-06-199816-4 (trade bdg.) — ISBN 978-0-06-199817-1 (lib. bdg.)

Design by Martha Rago and Rachel Zegar

11 12 13 14 15   LP/WOR   10 9 8 7 6 5 4 3 2 1

❖

First Edition

For you

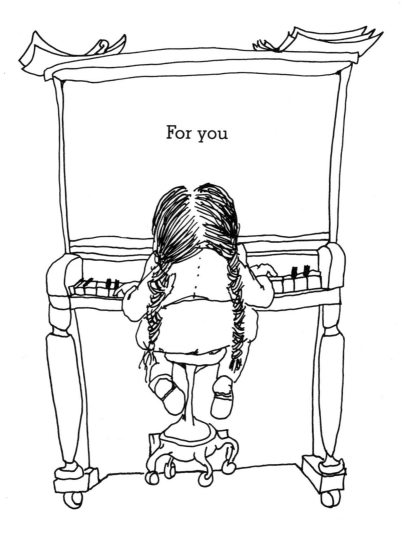

Every
Thing
On
It

YEARS FROM NOW

Although I cannot see your face
As you flip these poems awhile,
Somewhere from some far-off place
I hear you laughing—and I smile.

EVERY THING ON IT

I asked for a hot dog
With *everything* on it,
And that was my big mistake,
'Cause it came with a parrot,
A bee in a bonnet,
A wristwatch, a wrench, and a rake.
It came with a goldfish,
A flag, and a fiddle,
A frog, and a front porch swing,
And a mouse in a mask—
That's the last time I ask
For a hot dog with *everything*.

MY ZOOOTCH

I never have nightmares,
I'm happy to say.
The Zoootch on my bed
Always scares 'em away.

THE ONE WHO INVENTED TRICK OR TREAT

Yes, I invented "trick or treat"
So you could fill your mouth with sweets—
Candy bars and lemon drops,
Marshmallows and Tootsie Pops,
Butterscotch and bubble gum.
Hold out your hand—they'll give you some
Chocolate kisses, Jujubes,
Sourballs and jelly beans.
Have a cake—some cookies too.
Take a couple—grab a few
Peppermint sticks and Mary Janes,
Licorice whips and candy canes.
Slurp some soda, munch a pie,
Don't let those M&M's go by,
Chew that toffee, munch those treats,
Get that caramel in your teeth.
Then come see me, I'll be here—
I'm your friendly dentist, dear.

ALL PACKED

Me and Joe, we're all packed up,
Me and Joe, we've got our tickets,
Me and Joe, we're set to go—
Hey, wait a minute . . .
Where's Joe?

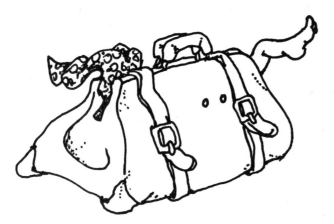

TOO SOON

You've spilt your milk
And dumped the mashed
Potatoes in your chair.
There's tapioca in your nose
And broccoli in your hair.
Your applesauce is on the wall
And nothin's on your spoon.
I think perhaps we let you
Try to feed yourself too soon.

THE GENIE IN THE FLASK

I opened up that magic flask,
And *zoof*, up popped a genie.
I thought he'd be my slave, but no—
This genie is a *meanie*.
Instead of filling every wish
And doing all my bidding,
He says that I must be *his* slave,
And oh, he isn't kidding.
I sweat and cough with no days off
From Tuesdays until Mondays.
I cook his beans and scrub his back
And wash his yucky undies
And sweep *and* paint—this surely ain't
The magic I was hopin'.
I guess in life it all depends
Which magic flask you open.

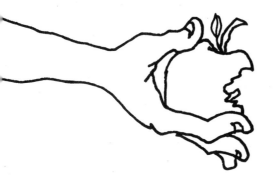

APPLE WITH ONE BITE MISSING

This apple's giving me the blues—
I'll sell it cheaply if you choose.
The fact is that it's slightly used
And I won't try to hide it.

It's red and sweet as it can be,
It's missing just one bite, you see,
And I can safely guarantee
There's half a worm inside it.

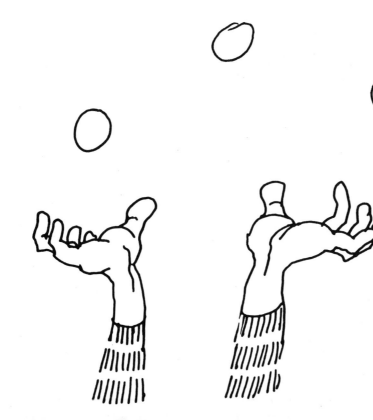

THE JUGGLER

The juggler is juggling an egg,
And now he is juggling two.
Now lookee, he
Is juggling *three*.
That's a very hard juggle to do.
And now one more—
That's number *four*,
Four flying eggs and then . . .
It's FIVE . . . now SIX . . . now SEVEN . . . *KAPLISH!*
We're back to *one* again. . . .

MASKS

She had blue skin,
And so did he.
He kept it hid
And so did she.
They searched for blue
Their whole life through,
Then passed right by—
And never knew.

HAPPY ENDING?

There are no happy endings.
Endings are the saddest part,
So just give me a happy middle
And a very happy start.

THIS HAT

What a silly-lookin' hat—
That's what everybody said.
What they don't realize

Is that . . .

. . . it exactly fits my head.

NEAL'S DEALS

Neal's deals, Neal's deals—
If you want a deal, come and see Neal.
Some of Neal's deals are really steals
And all of Neal's deals are really unreal.
He'll give you a deal on a non-swimming seal,
He'll give you a deal on a pig that won't squeal,
And if you'd like a no-engine automobile
Neal will make you a wonderful deal.

Neal's deals, Neal's deals—
You simply won't find better deals than Neal's.
He'll give you a deal on a boot with no heel,
He'll cut you a deal on a boat with no keel,
And if you'd consider a bike with one wheel,
Neal will make you a real sweet deal.

Neal's deals, deals by Neal—
Would you like a deal on this half-eaten meal?
You'd catch lots of fish with this old rusty reel,
And if you need a balloon made of steel
Or a bell that won't peal or a skunk named Camille,
Just come and see how terrific you feel
When you get a fabulous deal at Neal's.

ASLEEP

My lazy foot
Just fell asleep
When I sat down to sup.
I yelled and screamed,
But on it dreamed.
Well . . . *this* should wake it up.

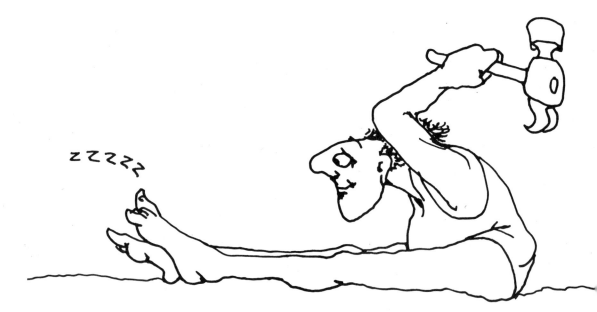

ZZZZZ

WALL MARKS

Those scratchy marks there on the wall,
They show how short I used to be.
They rise until they get this tall,
And Mama keeps reminding me
The way my dad would take his pen
And as I stood there, stiff and straight,
He'd put a ruler on my head
And mark the spot and write the date.
She says that it's my history,
But I don't understand at all
Just why she cries each time she sees
Those scratchy marks there on the wall.

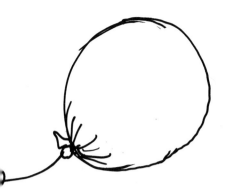

SANTA'S HELPER

I used to be Santa's helper,
But I got fired tonight.
Just 'cause I broke the music box
By windin' the spring too tight,
Just 'cause I tried all the bicycles
And licked all the candy canes,
Just 'cause I dropped those porcelain dolls
Down from the Tinker Toy crane,
Just 'cause I drove the 'lectric train
So fast it jumped the rails,
And wiped that purple finger paint
All over the sailboat sails,
And just 'cause I squeezed
The little stuffed dog
Till he gave a little stuffed yelp,
Santa had the nerve to say
I wasn't too much help.

A GIANT MISTAKE

A man he found a giant one day and stopped to have a look.
A man he found a giant one day, asleep beside a brook.
Around the giant's neck he tied a lengthy piece of twine.
Then he woke up the sleeping giant
And screamed,
"You're mine, you're mine!"
And there he stands in a hairy hand, but tell me if you can,
Does the man have the giant, or does the giant have the man?

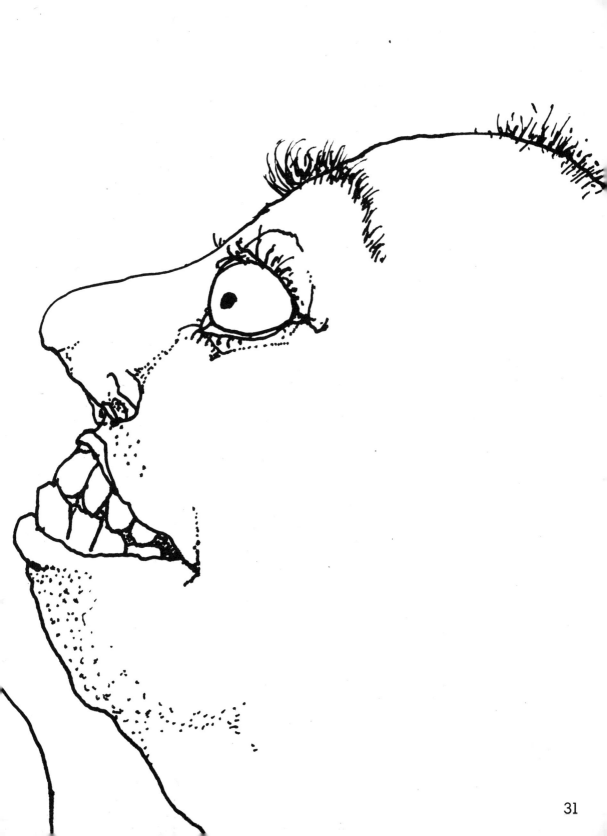

31

TRANSPARENT TIM

Transparent Timmy—
Maybe you knew him.
Everybody could
See right through him.
We saw his heart
Beatin' in there.
We saw his lungs
Breathin' air.
We saw his kidneys,
We saw his liver,
We saw his bones
And nerves aquiver.
We saw what he ate
For lunch today.
We saw the button
He lost last May.
But when we saw
Why his stomach hurt,
We made Tim
Put on his shirt.

ITCH

Please scratch my back and I'll make you rich.
I can't reach the place I itch.
Oo-ee-ooo, that feels so fine—
Thank you, friend, a million times.
Give you money? Why? What for?
I ain't itchin' anymore.

SHOT

I almost forgot
It's time for your shot.
It'll just take a second,
It won't hurt a lot.
So roll up or pull down
And we'll find the spot
For your shot.

PRO'S ADVICE

If you want to play tennis, I'll give you a tip:
You must practice your stroke,
You must tighten your grip,
You must straighten your shoulders
And swivel your hip
And develop your sense of sportsmanship.

LIZARD

A lizard in a blizzard
Got a snowflake in his gizzard
And nothing else much happened, I'm afraid,
But lizard rhymed with blizzard
And blizzard rhymed with gizzard
And that, my dear, is why most poems are made.

MUSTAR...

FOR THE WORLD'S RECORD

We made the world's longest hot dog,
And now that it's finally done,
We realize nobody's baked
The world's longest bun.

BOTTLE OPENER

Openin' bottles with my teeth—
They all called me funny.
Openin' bottles with my teeth—
Then they called me dummy.
Openin' bottles with my teeth—
Now they call me gummy.

A CAR WITH LEGS

A car with legs
Instead of wheels
Wears out soles
But never tires.
I'm sure that you
Can well afford her—
She's in perfect
Running order.

THE LOVETOBUTCANTS

I have a disease called
The "lovetobutcants"—
I think it's time I told it.
I'd love to help with that garbage can
But my fingers just can't hold it.
Hand me a bag of groceries and
My wrists just turn to jelly.
Cuttin' grass and hedges
Gives me flutters of the belly.
The smell of paint will make me faint,
Sweat makes my eyes start itchin'.
Dishwater on my little hands
Will start 'em shaky-twitchin'.
Pickin' clothes up off the floor
Would paralyze my shoulder.
I must not try to close a door,
At least not till I'm older.
So though I'd love to join the work—
Till this disease is done,
I'll have to lie here in the shade
While you have all the fun.

FINALLY

Hairy Harry Neverchop
At the age of ninety-two
Finally walked to a barber shop
And asked for a . . . *shampoo*.

STUBBORNNESS

There was a funky donkey and a spunky monkey.
They were sittin' by the railroad track.
Said the funky donkey to the spunky monkey,
"I'm goin' off to somewhere and I won't be back."
Said the spunky monkey to the funky donkey,
"If you wait for a minute or two,
I'll go say good-bye to the frivolous fly,
And I'll come along with you."

Said the spunky monkey to the funky donkey,
"This road looks long and wide,
So if you'll just pick me up and carry me awhile,
I'd sure be much obliged."
Said the funky donkey to the spunky monkey,
"I was gonna ask the same of you.
So we'd better just wait till we get it straight
As to who's gonna carry who."

Now the funky donkey he ain't goin' nowhere
'Less somebody carries him,
And the spunky monkey won't carry no donkey,
So their future's lookin' dim.
And they're still sittin' back by that railroad track.
They'll be there till the moon turns blue,
But they ain't gonna ride, 'cause they just can't decide
As to who's gonna carry who.

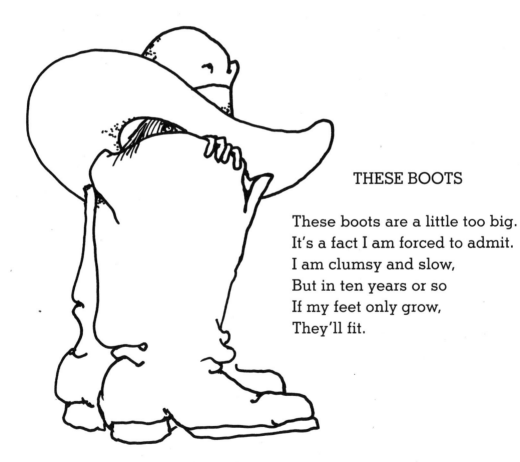

THESE BOOTS

These boots are a little too big.
It's a fact I am forced to admit.
I am clumsy and slow,
But in ten years or so
If my feet only grow,
They'll fit.

THE BALL GAME

The elephant played second base,
And the laughing hyena played third.
The two little leeches sat out in the bleachers,
Quite shocked by the language they heard.

The kangaroo leapt and the crocodile wept
Because they would not let him play.
And the ring-tailed rat, he kept swinging the bat
Till the poor bat flew up and away.

The spider was fit with a fielder's mitt,
But couldn't catch a fly at all,
As the octopus pitched and the hen sat and twitched
And tried to hatch the ball.

The porcupine umped and the kangaroo jumped
As the snail was out stealing third
On a throw from the snake just in time to awake
The sleeping Palatapus bird.

The trout, he struck out, but the yak took a whack
And hit one out into the lake.
A *homer* . . . it's *gone*. . . . No, the pelican yawned
And swallowed the ball by mistake.

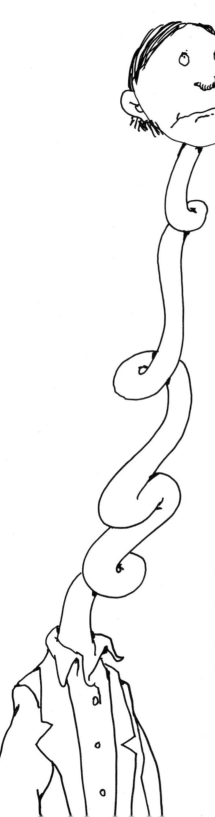

IN LOVE

If my face could only twist,
Then I could give my cheek a kiss
And whisper in my lovely ear,
"You're so beautiful, my dear,"
And look into my eyes and see
Just how much I'm in love with me.

48

HAPPY NEW

Joe yelled, "Happy New Year."
The cow yelled, "Happy Moo Year."
The ghost yelled, "Happy Boo Year."
The doctor yelled, "Happy Flu Year."
The penguin sneezed, "Happy Ah-choo Year."
The skunk yelled, "Happy Pee-yoo Year."
The owl hooted, "Happy Too-woo Year."
The cowboy yelled, "Happy Yahoo Year."
The trainman yelled, "Happy Choo-choo Year."
The clock man yelled, "Happy Cuckoo Year."
The barefoot man yelled, "Happy Shoe Year."
The hungry man said, "Happy Chew Year."
There were more "Happy Ooo-Years"
Than you ever heard
At our New Year's party . . .
Last June twenty-third.

DIRTY FEET

We had a dirty-foot contest
In the middle of Mudpuddle Street,
And all the unwashed dirty-foot kids
Came with their filthy feet.
There was Shoeless Billy and Toe-Jam Tillie
And the boy who walked through mustard.
There was Oozy-Toes Trish, who loved to squish
Her toes in lemon custard.
Through muck and mud, through slush and crud,
They came from coast to coast,
And we scraped the dirt off everyone's feet
To see whose weighed the most.
And Toe-Jam Tillie's weighed thirteen pounds,
But the winner was Sloppy-Sole Saul,
'Cause when they scraped all *his* foot dirt away,
There were no feet there at all.

SCHOOL

Rain and hail,
Cold and snow
Are good excuses not to go.

MAN-EATING PLANT

Has anyone here seen Mister Mo?
Said the man-eating plant, "We *did*."
Did he come in here an hour ago?
Said the man-eating plant, "He *did*."
He was carryin' Nugrow and potting pans
And chlorophyll boxes and waterin' cans,
And he came in here to feed the plants.
Said the man-eating plant, "He *did*."

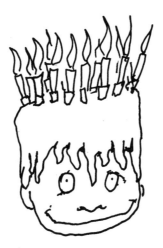

HAPPY BIRTHDAY

So what if nobody came?
I'll have *all* the ice cream and tea,
And I'll laugh with myself,
And I'll dance with myself,
And I'll sing, "Happy Birthday to me!"

FOURTH PLACE

I came in fourth in the beauty contest
(Please let me cry a minute).
I came in *fourth* in the beauty contest
(I was so *sure* I'd win it).
They can keep their ribbon that says fourth place
(And I don't care where they pin it).
I came in *fourth* in a beauty contest
And there were just *three* of us in it.

UNHAPPY HERE

Mail me somewhere,
Mail me somewhere,
Wrap me and pack me
And mail me somewhere.
Parcel Post, UPS,
Regular mail or Air,
All wrapped up in brown paper
That won't rip or tear,
With stamps on my forehead
And string in my hair,
And a tag on my butt that says
"Handle with care."
Paste on any address,
It don't matter where,
Illinois or Kentucky
Or Delaware.
'Cause wherever it is,
I'll be happier *there*—
So please *ship* me—*send* me—
Mail me somewhere.

GARLIC BREATH

Little Seth had garlic breath—
Said hi to his sister and breathed her to death.
Breathed on the grass
And the grass all died.
Breathed on an egg and the egg got fried.
Breathed on the air and the air turned green.
Breathed on the clock and it struck thirteen.
Breathed on the cat and the cat went moo.
Breathed on the cow and the cow gave glue.
Breathed on his brother,
His brother went blind.
Breathed on his mother
And she lost her mind.
Breathed on a top
And made it spin.
Breathed on the house
And the walls caved in.
Breathed on his feet and they ran from Seth,
Just to get away from his garlic breath.

THE ROMANCE

Said the pelican to the elephant,
"I think we should marry, I do.
'Cause there's no name that rhymes with me
And no one else rhymes with you."

Said the elephant to the pelican,
"There's sense to what you've said,
For rhyming's as good a reason as any
For any two to wed."

And so the elephant wed the pelican,
And they dined upon lemons and limes,
And now they have a baby pelicant
And everybody rhymes.

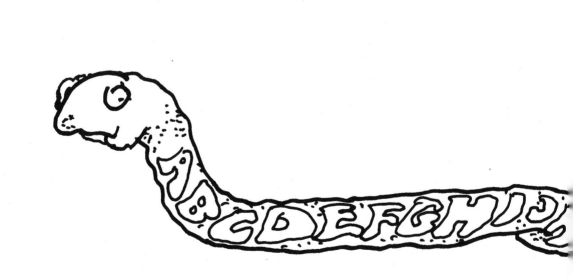

OUCH!

If you're learnin' to read
But you haven't learned yet,
And the B's and the D's
Are just givin' you fits,
And you feel about twenty-six
Pains where you sit,
It's that ol' Letter Snake—
You've been alpha-bit.

BEE

Instead of this dumb spelling bee
Why don't they hold a yelling bee?
A screaming bee, a hitting bee,
A nagging bee, a spitting bee,
A jumping bee, a leaping bee,
A whining bee, a sleeping bee?
A bee where you just twirl and spin—
And then maybe *I'd* have a chance to win.

TURNING INTO

Swingin' from
A hick'ry bough,
I felt so brave
I hollered . . .

WOW

But down I fell
Just like a bomb.
And I heard my "wow"
Turn into . . .

YESEES AND NOEES

The Yesees said yes to anything
That anyone suggested.
The Noees said no to everything
Unless it was proven and tested.
So the Yesees all died of much too much
And the Noees all died of fright,
But somehow I think the Thinkforyourselfees
All came out all right.

TINY FOOTPRINTS

See the tiny footprints
Leadin' through the snow.
Follow tiny footprints—
Soon you're gonna know
(If you escape the snapping beak
And the flapping wings)
Tiny footprints are not always
Made by tiny things.

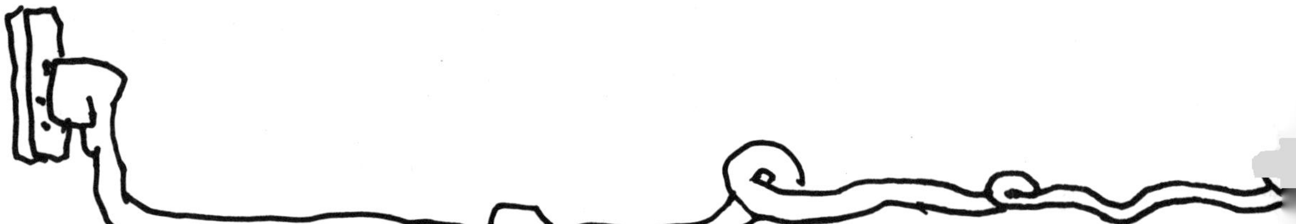

WHOOSH

My hair blower worked in *reverse* today—
There's really not much more to say.

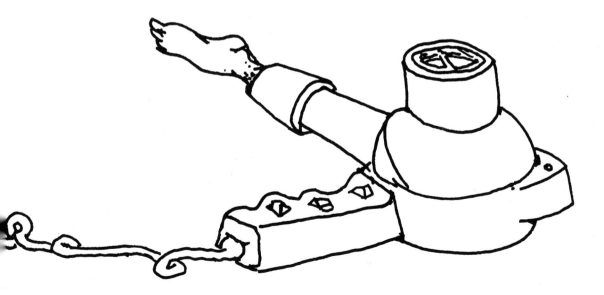

A MOUSE IN THIS HOUSE

"There's a mouse in this house," said Uncle Ben
As he peeked down a hole in the floor.
"There's a mouse in this house," he said again
As he pushed aside the chest of drawers.
"A mouse in this house," he cried once more
As he ripped down the drapes in the hall
And pulled up the boards in the kitchen floor
And hammered a hole in the dining-room wall.
He yanked all the pictures right off their hooks,
Pushed over the bookcase, and tore through the books.
"A mouse," he rasped as he searched around,
"In this house," he gasped as a beam came down.
He dug through the closets, he poked through the trash.
The overhead ceiling fan fell with a crash.
He pried up the tiles, he chopped up the hose
(He was *sure* that he saw a mouse's nose).
He jerked all the bathroom drainpipes out,
Unscrewed all the faucets, and looked up the spouts.
"Is that a switch or a mouse's ear?"
Down came the dining-room chandelier.
"A mouse in this house," we heard him shout,
As he got his chainsaw out.

He sawed through the baseboards,
He sawed through the struts,
He poked through the plaster
As he sliced and he cut
All the 'lectrical wires that ran through the house
(They *did* look a bit like the tail of a mouse).
He tore down the banister and pulled up the nails
(A mouse can hide down under banister rails).
He sliced through the carpet, he ripped up the stairs,
He sawed through the table and splintered the chairs.
Now what was that?—on the windowsill?
He got out his hydraulic drill.
Crack went the windows—*zip* went the screens.
Down fell the ceiling—down came the beams.
He tore up the cement and the stone cellar, too.
He smashed in the fireplace and looked up the flue,
Dug out the foundation from under the house
Mutterin' somethin' 'bout "some lousy mouse,"
Yankin' the hinges right off the doors,
Bashin' down rafters and two-by-fours,
And then, as the last of the walls caved in,
A small gray tail flicked out of sight
Right past the shoe of Uncle Ben.
"Aha," he whispered, "I was right."

THREE FLAMINGOS

Who ate the S's right out of my name?
Without any S's it's just not the same.
What a horrible crime—what a sin—what a shame,
And I really don't know just who is to blame.

THE RACE

If you rode a turtle
And I rode a snail
And we raced to the equator,
One of us would come in last
And one would come in later.

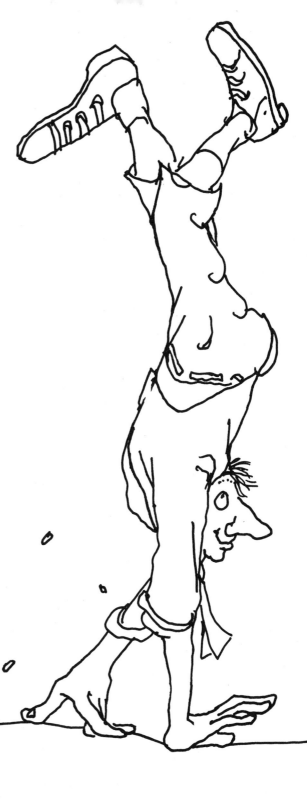

GOOD IDEA

Try to get Dad
To walk on his hands,
Then clap and cheer,
"Oh, do some more!"
So there he goes proudly,
And now's your chance
To pick up the change
That fell out on the floor.

THE SCIENTIST
AND THE HIPPOPOTAMUS?

You just can't believe
Everything that they tell you
Just 'cause they teach it
And preach it and shout.
They say you can't eat nothin'
Bigger than you are. . . .
You've really got to check
These things out.

GROWING DOWN

Mix a grunt and a grumble, a sneer and a frown,
And what do you have? Why old Mr. Brown,
The crabbiest man in our whole darn town.
We all called him Grow-Up Brown:
For years each girl and boy and pup
Heard "Grow up, grow up, oh grow up."
He'd say, '"Why don't you be polite?
Why must you shout and fuss and fight?
Why can't you keep dirt off your clothes?
Why can't you remember to wipe your nose?
Why must you always make such noise?
Why don't you go pick up your toys?
Why do you hate to wash your hands?
Why are your shoes all filled with sand?
Why must you shout when I'm lying down?
Why don't you grow up?" grumped Grow-Up Brown.

One day we said to Grow-Up Brown,
"Hey, why don't you try growing down?
Why don't you crawl on your knees?
Why don't you try climbing trees?
Why don't you bang on a tin-can drum?
Why don't you chew some bubble gum?
Why don't you play kick-the-can?
Why don't you *not* wash your hands?
Why don't you join the baseball team?
Why don't you jump and yell and scream?
Why don't you try skipping stones?
Why don't you eat ice cream cones?

Why don't you cry when you feel sad?
Why don't you cuddle with your dad?
Why don't you have weenie roasts?
Why don't you believe in ghosts?
Why don't you have pillow fights?
Why don't you sleep with your teddy at night?
Why don't you swing from monkey bars?
Why don't you wish on falling stars?
Why don't you run in three-legged races?
Why don't you make weirdie faces?
Why don't you smile, Grow-Up Brown?
Why don't you try growing down?"
Then Grow-Up Brown, he scrunched and frowned
And scratched his head and walked around,
And finally he said with a helpless sound,
"Maybe I will try growing down."

So Grow-Up Brown began to sing
And started doing silly things:
He started making weirdie faces
And came in first in the three-legged races.
All day he swung from monkey bars,
All night he'd lie and count the stars.
He tooted horns, he banged on drums,
He spent twenty bucks on bubble gum,
He went to all the weenie roasts,
And once he thought he saw a ghost.
He got to be great at pillow fights
And went to sleep with his teddy at night.
He flew a kite, he kicked a can,
He rubbed some dirt upon his hands.

He drew some pictures, threw some stones,
Ate forty-seven ice cream cones.
He got some sand between his toes,
Got a loose tooth and a bloody nose.
He got a dog, they rolled in the mud.
He imitated Elmer Fudd.
He climbed a roof (though no one asked),
He broke his wrist—he wore a cast.
He rolled down hills, he climbed up trees,
He scuffed his elbows, skinned his knees,
He tried to join the baseball team;
When they said no, he spit and screamed.
He cried when he was feeling sad
And went and cuddled with his dad.
He wore a hat that didn't fit,
He learned just how far he could spit,
He learned to wrestle and get tickled,
Sucked his thumb, he belched and giggled.
He got his trousers torn and stained,
He ran out barefoot in the rain,
Shouting to all the folks in town,
"It's much more fun, this growin' down."

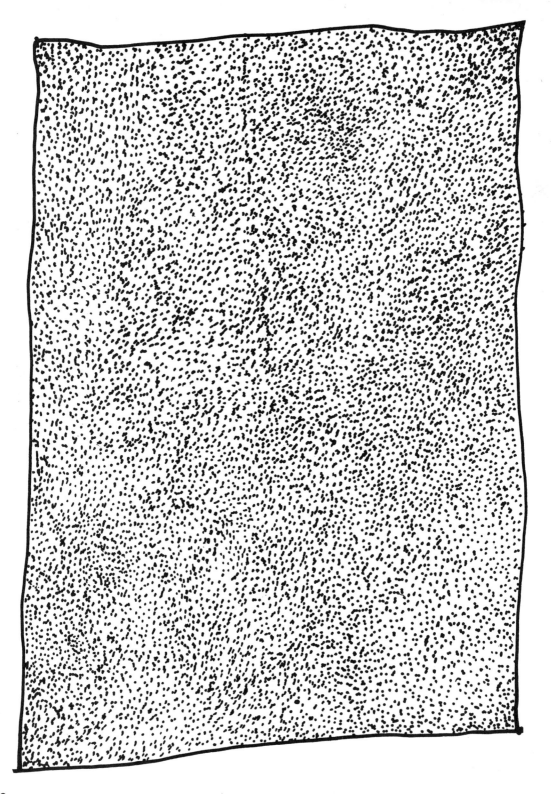

80

THE FROG

And here's a bashful frog
Hiding 'hind a log
In a muddy bog
In a very heavy fog.

LOVE IS GRAND BUT . . .

Miz' Pelican said she loved me,
And to show how much she cared,
She let me set inside her beak
And took me flyin' everywhere.
But then—below—she spied a fish
And dove—and let me fall—*cr-unch*,
As she whispered, "Love is grand,
But lunch, my dear, is lunch."

HOW HUNGRY IS POLLY?

"I'm so hungry I could eat a horse,"
Said Polly in the park.
Ol' Dobbin, grazin' nearby,
Overheard her rude remark.
He shook his mane and pawed the ground,
He raised his noble head,
He snorted and looked down at her,
And this is what he said:
"I've been ridden, I've been driven,
I've been raced around a track,
I've been photographed with little
Whiny kiddies on my back.
I've pulled wagons through the winter,
I've pulled sleighs and I've pulled sleds,
I've pulled plows in sticky summers
With flies buzzin' 'round my head.
I've been whipped and I've been beaten,
I've been called a such-and-such—
But to think of being eaten,
Well, that really is too much!
And when I get insulted,
My appetite runs wild,
And now I feel so hungry,
I could eat a *child*."

TWENTY-EIGHT USES FOR SPAGHETTI

Spaghetti has so many uses,
It can be used for whips or nooses,
It makes great backstraps for papooses,
Or leashes, when you're walking gooses.
It makes a perfect slingshot sling,
It makes a great cat's cradle string,
A jumpin' rope, a scooter tire,
A bouncy acrobatic wire,
A boxing ring, where you can spar,
Six twangy strings for your guitar.
And though it's droopy, warm, and wet,
It makes a lovely tennis net.
And as suspenders it's just fine
For holdin' pants up (yours, not *mine*).
A string to fly your red balloon,
A phone cord for your telephoon,
Hair ribbons, neckties, or boot laces,
Reindeer reins for reindeer races,
A wig to fit a silly queen,
A mushy beard for Halloween.
And it can make a neat lasso.
In fact, there's nothin' it *can't* do.
Oh—and you can *eat* it too.

I DID KNOT

Somebody tied a knot
In the snake
While he was sleepin'. . . .
Now he's awake.

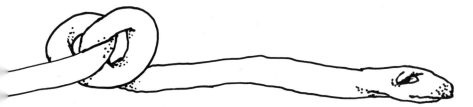

JIMMY-JACK-JOHN

"Oh, where are you goin', my Jimmy-Jack-John,
With only the moon for your light?"
    "I'm goin' 'round in search of the dawn,
    And I'll prob'ly be gone most the night."

"Oh, why are you cryin', my Jimmy-Jack-John,
And why do you stare out to sea?"
    "I'm thinkin' that over the waves of the pond
    The dawn lies a-waitin' for me."

"But why do you wander, my Jimmy-Jack-John,
A-roamin' in search of the blue?
Just wrap yourself tight in this blanket of night
And the dawn will come to you."

HOUSEBROKEN

The puppy's housebroken at last?
Lord only knows he was needin' it.
You've trained him to go
On the newspaper? Fine.
But please—not while I'm readin' it.

WRONG WAY

This is *not* what I asked for,
This is *not* what I'd planned
When I said, "Okay,
You can bury me
Up to my neck in the sand."

THE CLOCK MAN

"How much will you pay for an extra day?"
The clock man asked the child.
"Not one penny," the answer came,
"For my days are as many as smiles."

"How much will you pay for an extra day?"
He asked when the child was grown.
"Maybe a dollar or maybe less,
For I've plenty of days of my own."

"How much will you pay for an extra day?"
He asked when the time came to die.
"All of the pearls in all of the seas,
And all of the stars in the sky."

WRITESINGTELLDRAW

I've told you a hundred tall stories,
I've sung you a thousand sweet songs,
I've wrote you a million ridiculous rhymes
(Though sometimes the grammar was wrong).
I've drawn you a zillion pictures,
So being as fair as can be,
After all that I've writtensungtolddrawn for you,
Won't you writesingtelldraw one for me?

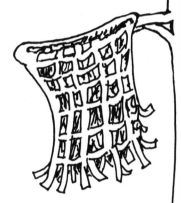

SLAM DUNKER

Short guys *can* play basketball—
You really don't have to be seven feet tall
If you got the want-to and you got the try
(And you got a basket that's four feet high).

THE PELICAN

Pickin' big fish from the seas
The pelican can do with ease,
But pickin' up a tiny ant
Is something that a peli*cant.*

TRAMPOLINE

Bouncin' upon the trampoline
So high above the ground,
Just as I was goin' up
I saw her—comin' down.

She had a daisy in her hair,
She wore a silken gown,
But when she started goin' up,
I was comin' down.

I tried to say, "Hello—nice day."
She smiled and spun around.
"Come up awhile with me," yelled she,
But I was goin' down.

And so, as yet, we've never met
Because we've sadly found
That one is always goin' up
While one is comin' down.

MY HAT

Some wear berets and some wear fedoras,
Some like sombreros a lot.
Some prefer caps with those floppity flaps
And those little propellers on top.
Some wear fancy high hats,
And some like the kind that's
Got duck bills or Mickey Mouse ears.
But why is it that when I put on my hat,
Everyone just disappears?

THE DANCE OF THE SHOES

Were you there for the dance of the shoes
When they skipped in a column of twos—
From the closet they crept
And they jumped, skipped, and leapt
Doin' the dance of the shoes:
And the high heels clicked
And the football cleats kicked
And the sandals flip-flopped
And the clogs clipped and clopped
And the button shoes creaked
And the sneakers just sneaked
And the baby shoes skipped
And the slippers both slipped
And the ballet shoes jumped
And the hunting shoes clumped?
They started at seven and danced until ten,
When they all tiptoed back to the closet again.
Oh the dance of the shoes,
Now they stand in a row
Lookin' proper and right
And actin' just like
They've been there all night.

INVESTIGATING

Professor Shore, from Memphis State,
Decided to investigate
Just how the elephant's tail was tied
Onto the elephant's leathery hide.
Well, while he was investigating,
Something happened, so nauseating
And so disgusting that I fear it
Just might make you sick to hear it.
So let's just say Professor Shore
Doesn't investigate tails no more.
(You'll find surprises happen mostly
When we investigate too closely.)

IN HER . . .

In her long mink coat
And her buckskin pants
And her lizard-skin boots
With the rattlesnake bands
And her beaver hat
With the raccoon tails
We heard her shoutin' . . .

HE TRIED TO HIDE

He dreamed of a glunk with a horrible face
And thought he'd better *hide* someplace.
He tried to hide between the sheets
And found an ogre with two left feet.
He tried to hide in the dresser drawer
And heard a hungry tiger roar.
He tried to hide beneath the bed
And found a body without a head.
He tried to hide behind the door
And heard a sleeping monster snore.
He tried to hide down in the basement
And found a dragon to his amazement.
He tried to hide beneath the stair
And found a mummy grinnin' there.
He tried to hide behind the drapes
And found a dozen hairy apes.
He tried to hide behind a dresser
And found a murderin' mad professor.
He tried to hide in a pile of clothes
And found a witch with a warty nose.
He tried to hide under the sink
And found a vampire takin' a drink.
He tried to hide in the garbage pail
And found a werewolf sharpenin' his nails.
So he went back to bed, that's what he did,
And he dreamed of tomorrow,
And *there* he hid.

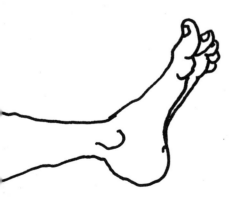

HOLDING

We can't hold hands—
Someone might see.
Won't you please
Hold toes with me?

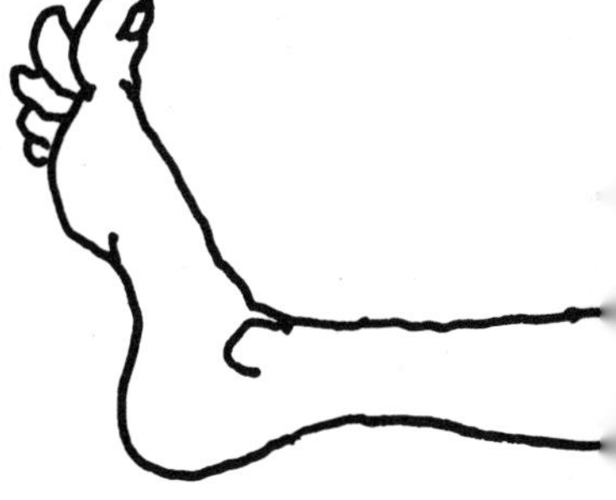

WHY I'M SCREAMIN'

The dentist tried to pull my tooth out.
He pulled but couldn't get the root out.
He pulled that tooth right out the door,
He pulled it down to Baltimore.
He took the train to Hackensack,
He booked a plane to Fond du Lac.
He hitched a ride to Santa Fe,
He hired a guide to San Jose,
He swam across the Windsor Straits,
He zipped through Maine on roller skates.
He poled a raft down Frenchman's Crick,
He bounced through Nome on a pogo stick.
He sailed a boat through Puget Sound,
He rode a goat through Provincetown,
And now he's pedalin' through Duluth,
Still pullin' on that stubborn tooth.
And he's chargin' me all the while
Not by the *tooth*—but by the *mile*.

TIC-TAC-TOE

Let's play tic-tac-toe.
I'll take the X's,
You take the—*OH*—
Sticking a tack in someone's toe
Is not the way to play, you know.

FRIGHTENED

"There are *kids* underneath my bed,"
Cried little baby monster Fred.
Momma monster smiled. "Oh, Fred,
There's no such thing as kids," she said.

LOSING PIECES

Talked my head off
Worked my tail off
Cried my eyes out
Walked my feet off
Sang my heart out
So you see,
There's really not much left of me.

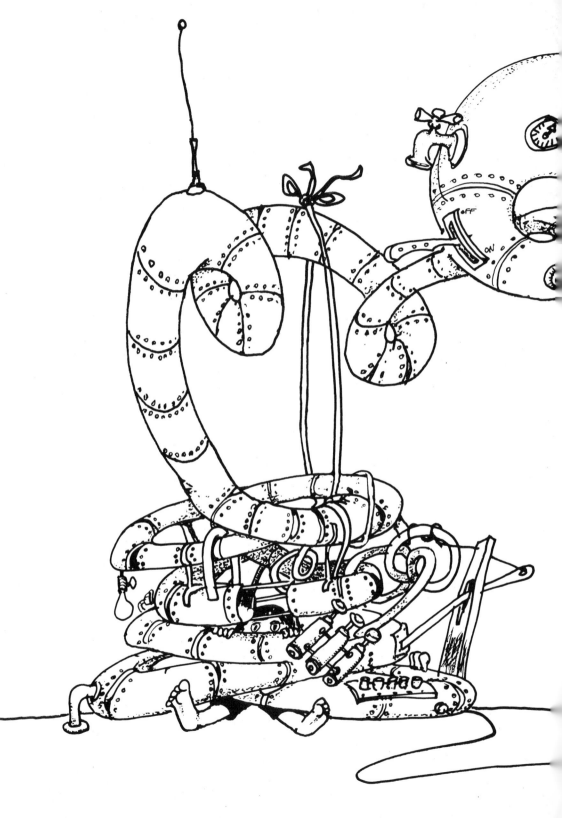

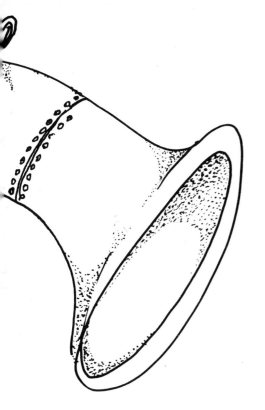

HORN

It's a highly unusual horn.
I bought it from Hustlin' Paul.
He said if I practice five minutes a day,
I'll be great in just no time at all.
And soon I'll give concerts for princes and kings,
Playing as sweet as the nightingale sings,
As soft as the snow falls,
As clear as the rain,
As loud as the wild winds of winter,
And they'll all love my music once I figure out
Which end of this thing you blow inter.

MISTAKE

Please don't ask me
What and where
And how and why and when.
Let's just say
I took a dare
And I don't think I'll do it again.

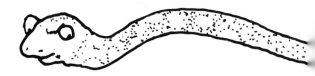

B.L. . . . WHAT?

Dog, how could you do this to me?
Eat the tomato out of my B.L.T.
I'm mad and hungry as I can be.
I just might make a B.L.*D.*

THE UGLY CONTEST

The Ugly Contest is ready to begin—
First come the ones with the sharp pointy chins,
Now come the ones with the big toothless grins,
Now come the fish faces shaking their fins,
Now come the ones with their eyeballs sunk in,
Now come the creeps from the old garbage bin,
Now come the ones with the green, scaly skin,
Now come the scuzzies and all of their kin,
Now comes you . . . you win!

THE GAME

I'm glad you came.
Let's play a game
Called Crook and Police Dog Rover.
I bite your eye,
And now you die,
And now the game is over.

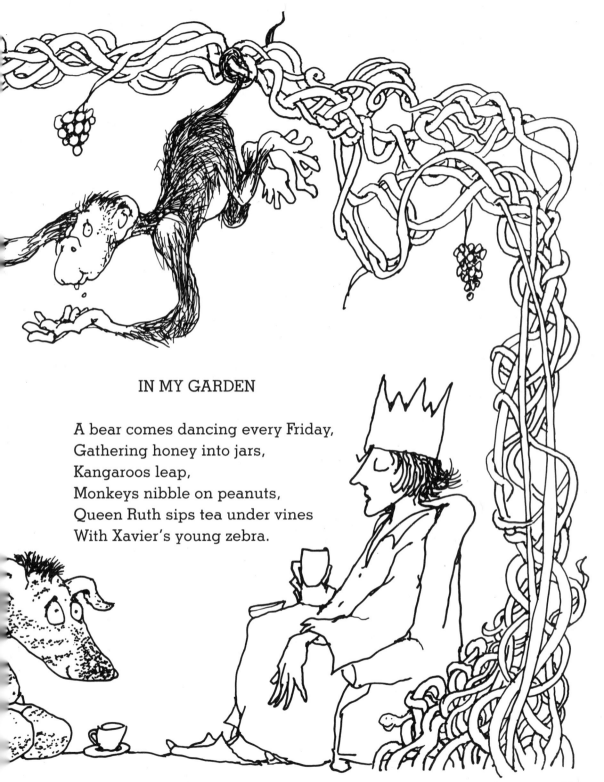

IN MY GARDEN

A bear comes dancing every Friday,
Gathering honey into jars,
Kangaroos leap,
Monkeys nibble on peanuts,
Queen Ruth sips tea under vines
With Xavier's young zebra.

I'VE GOT YOUR NOSE

She yelled, "I've got your nose,"
And squeezed her fingers 'round her thumb.
She thought it was cute, I suppose—
I thought it was silly and stupid and dumb.
But then I looked into the mirror
And got such a scare.
She *did*! She *did*! She took my *nose*
And left her *finger* there.

SUPERSTAR

I'm the greatest newest superstar,
And soon you'll cheer my name.
I'm smart and slick and strong and quick,
An expert at the game.
But 'fore we start, one question, please.
I hesitate to ask it,
But . . . where's the basket?

CHANGING THE BABY

We like to change the baby
Every time he cries.
We like to change the baby—
Why are you surprised?
We like to change the baby,
Don't ask me how or why.
But we'd like to change the baby—
For one that's always dry.

SIGN

This means victory,
This means peace,
It also means
Two hamburgers please.

THE STAIRWAY

I climbed the stairway to the sun
To fill my eyes with burning gold.
But oh the sky was dank and dark,
And there the air was damp and cold,
And down below the earth shone bright.
I sat and stared in wonder. Then,
I crawled back down—I don't think I
Will climb those stairs again.

BIOGRAPHY

First he was born,
And then he was warned,
And then he was taught how to swim,
And then he was married,
And then he was buried,
And that's all that happened to him.

FRED'S HEADS

Fred's Heads—that's what the sign said.
Want a new head? Come see Fred.
Find the head that fits you best.
Leave your own with all the rest.
Try on one of sunny smiles,
Wear this one that cries awhile.
Here is one that whistles and winks,
Here is one that frowns and thinks.
How about this one that grins?
When you find it's wearin' thin,
Bring it back and trade it in.

B. ↓ O.
R. R.

ENGINEER

MUSTACHE MO

Mustache Mo of the B. & O.—
His mustache grows ten feet or so.
It got caught in the wheels below.
Now there's no mustache
And no mo' Mo.

NASTY NANCY'S STORE

Whatever you want we're all out of.
Whatever you need we ain't got.
If you ask if we have what you heard that we have,
I'll tell you right now we do *not*.
We're sold out of what-you-come-in-for.
No, we only sell that now and then.
No, we don't carry *those*
And we're already closed—
Our hours are from 12:00 to 12:10.

I DIDN'T

I didn't do it
That's a lie
I didn't do it
No, not I
I didn't do it
Hear me cry
I didn't do it
Hope to die
I didn't do it
I'm not that bad
But if I *did* . . .
Would you be mad?

UNDERFACE

Underneath my outside face
There's a face that none can see.
A little less smiley,
A little less sure,
But a whole lot more like me.

CALL THE PLEASE

The Police Department
Changed their garments
And became the *Please* Department.
And instead of clubs and cuffs,
Saying Please was quite enough.
"Please stop breaking down that door."
"Please stop robbing that jewelry store."
"Please stop smashing that computer."
"Please stop stealing that motor scooter."
"Please stop shooting off that gun."
"Please stop forging checks for fun."
"Please stop ripping off those tires."
"Please stop setting things on fire."
And if they needed more persuasion,
They took 'em down to the Please Station
Where the friendly Chief of Please
Said Please, Please, Please
On bended knees.
And they stopped all crime with ease
By politely saying "Please."
So the next time that you're feelin' blue
'Cause someone points a gun at you
While they're robbin' your apartment,
Just call your friendly Please Department.

NOT AN EGG

With feathers blue and comb of red,
With claws that scrape and scratch,
The Rhymey Bird sits on my head
And waits for it to hatch.
"It's not an egg," I cry, but she
Sets waitin' for the day
When it will *crack*, and with a shout
A baby poem will tumble out
And shake its feathers all about
And flap . . . and fly away.

THE RAINBOW THROWER

The rainbow thrower
Squints his eye
And hurls his colors
'Cross the sky
While far beyond
Horizon's gate
The rainbow catcher
Sits and waits.

BEFORE THE RACE

Mr. Flack tells his son Jack,
"Run hard—with no excuses."
Mr. Brill tells his son Will
He'll kill him if he loses.
Mr. Drew tells little Lou
"Be fearless but beware,"
And little Trace, he *won* the race
(*His* father wasn't *there*).

WALENDA THE WITCH

Walenda is the *weirdest* witch—
And maybe you have seen her.
She uses her broom to sweep her room—
And flies on her vacuum cleaner.

CINDERELLA

She left the palace,
She left the dance,
Left one of her
Shoes behind her.
I don't know,
But at a glance—
I don't think
I'll try to find her.

AFTER

After the snowmelt and after the rain,
Out of the ground a hand came
And drew me a picture
And wrote me a poem
And touched my face gently
And pointed me home.

FOUR GIRL PONY

Just 'cause Gail's got short spiked hair
She gets to be the head of the horse.
Just 'cause Jane's got a long red mane
She gets to be the neck, of course.
Just 'cause Di is very shy
She gets to be the horse's spine.
And just 'cause I've got a ponytail
I've got to be the horse's behind.

OPENIN' NIGHT

She had the jitters
She had the flu
She showed up late
She missed her cue
She kicked the director
She screamed at the crew
And tripped on a prop
And fell in some goo
And ripped her costume
A place or two
Then she forgot
A line she knew
And went "Meow"
Instead of "Moo"
She heard 'em giggle
She heard 'em boo
The programs sailed
The popcorn flew
As she stomped offstage
With a boo-hoo-hoo
The fringe of the curtain
Got caught in her shoe
The set crashed down
The lights did too
Maybe that's why she didn't want to do
An interview.

HENRY HALL

Henry Hall
Moved here last fall.
Henry Hall
Is strong and tall.
Henry Hall
Outjumps us all.
Give Henry Hall
The basketball.
He'd rip the basket
Off the wall.
The others all
Would surely fall
When Henry Hall
Would shoot the ball.
We'd win 'em all
With Henry Hall.
But Henry Hall . . .
Hates basketball.

P.S. The one in the hat is Henry Hall.
The one on the left is Clumsy Paul.
We hardly let him play at all.

MILKING TIME

Nearsighted Norman took his pail
And went to milk the bull.
He sat on his stool,
He rolled up his sleeves
And gave the tail a pull.
The bull gave a snort
And a twist of his horns . . .
Has anyone sighted
Ol' Nearsighted Norm?

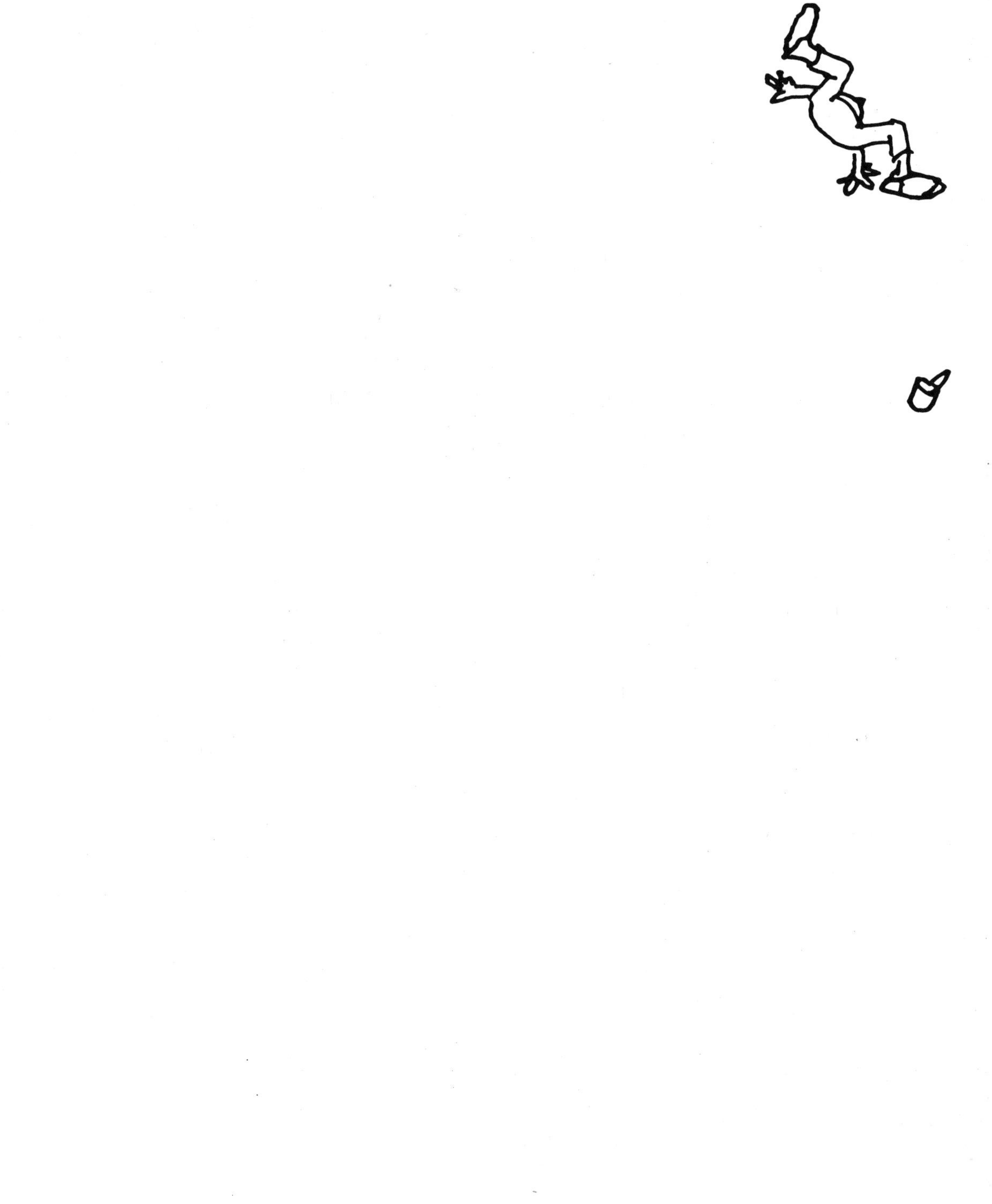

DON'T CHANGE ON MY ACCOUNT

If you're sloppy, that's just fine.
If you're moody, I won't mind.
If you're fat, that's fine with me.
If you're skinny, let it be.
If you're bossy, that's all right.
If you're nasty, I won't fight.
If you're rough, well that's just you.
If you're mean, that's all right too.
Whatever you are is all okay.
I don't like you anyway.

DIRTY CLOTHES

Some put 'em in a washer,
Some toss 'em in a tub,
Some dump 'em in a laundry truck
For someone else to scrub.
Some stick 'em in a hamper,
Some stuff 'em in a sack.
I never worry 'bout 'em—
I just keep 'em on my back.

DUMB

The dumbest thing
That any kid
Could ever do
I did.

RUDE RUDY REESE

Rude Rudy Reese, Rude Rudy Reese,
He never said Thank you
And never said Please.
He'd yell, "Gimme a quarter,"
Or "Cook me some peas,"
Or "Pass me the salt"
(But he never said Please).
One day, down the mountain
He came on his skis,
Yellin', "Clear me a path."
(But he never said Please.)
So he bounced off the rocks
And got caught in the trees,
Yellin', "Help get me down"
(But he didn't say Please).
So he tried climbin' down,
But he slipped on some leaves,
Yellin', "Catch me, someone"
(But he didn't say Please).

So he fell in some poo
Right up to his knees,
Yellin', "Quick, pull me out"
(But he didn't say Please).
Then he got attacked
By some low-flyin' geese.
(We'd have shooed 'em away,
But he didn't say Please.)
So he sunk to his chin,
Then along came some bees.
He screamed, "Throw me a rope"
(But he didn't say Please).
Then along came a reptile
From out of the seas.
(He thought Lord, save me now,
But he didn't think Please.)
So the reptile ate him
With crackers and cheese.
(We'd have passed *him* the salt,
But he didn't say Please.)

NEW JOB

Just two hours workin' in the candy store
And I don't like candy anymore.

THE DOLLHOUSE

You can't crawl back in the dollhouse—
You've gotten too big to get in.
You've got to live here
Like the rest of us do.
You've got to walk roads
That are winding and new.
But oh, I wish I could
Crawl back with you,
Into the dollhouse again.

YOU'LL NEVER BE KING

You'll never be king, said the queen to the prince,
If you keep on misplacing your crown,
And you twirl your scepter just like a baton
And you walk through the halls upside down.

He'll never be king, said the duke to the earl,
For he plays with his toes on the throne,
And he wiggles and giggles and rolls in the mud
And he likes to go walking alone.

Oh I shall be king, said the prince to himself,
And my people shall all learn to sing
And play in the sand and walk on their hands
And have as much fun as their king!

GOING UP, GOING DOWN

A skinny, hungry alligator
Got in a crowded elevator.
The doors slid shut,
And six floors later,
A fat and burping alligator
Got off an empty elevator.

ITALIAN FOOD

Oh, how I love Italian food.
I eat it all the time,
Not just 'cause how good it tastes
But 'cause how good it rhymes.
Minestrone, cannelloni,
Macaroni, rigatoni,
Spaghettini, scallopini,
Escarole, braciole,
Insalata, cremolata, manicotti,
Marinara, carbonara,
Shrimp francese, Bolognese,
Ravioli, mostaccioli,
Mozzarella, tagliatelle,
Fried zucchini, rollatini,
Fettuccine, green linguine,
Tortellini, Tetrazzini,
Oops—I think I split my jeani.

LOOKING FOR SANTA

They told me once and I didn't believe—
You won't see him comin', you won't see him leave.
So I'll tell you once, and you'd better believe—
Don't look up the chimney on Christmas Eve.

STICK-A-TONGUE-OUT SID

Did you hear about Stick-a-Tongue-Out Sid?
He stuck out his tongue at all the kids.
He stuck it out at recess and then
At lunch he stuck it out again.
School days he stuck it out at his teacher,
Sundays he stuck it out at the preacher.
Saturdays he stuck it out at a double feature.
But one day he stuck it out at Helen McHatter,
A girl who didn't like tongues stuck out at 'er.
She grabbed that tongue, she pulled it hard,
She rolled it out about twenty yards
And danced around, and 'round and 'round,
And 'round and 'round, that tongue unwound
Around his head, around his chin,
Around his neck and back again,
She wound it once around his eyes,
Around his ears she wound it twice,
Around his face she wrapped it light,
Around his waist she wrapped it tight.
Around his back, around his seat,
Around his legs, around his feet,
Until he stood there—all entwined
With no more tongue left to unwind.
And now Stick-a-Tongue-Out Sid
Really is a tongue-tied kid.

NASTY SCHOOL

Oh have you heard of nasty school?
They teach nasty things and they have nasty rules.
They only take nasties and rowdies and fools,
So come, let's take a walk through nasty school.
You get to nasty school through a secret gate.
The first rule is you must be late.
Your hands and face must be all caked with dirt.
There must be lots of grease and gravy spots upon your shirt.
In class, instead of listening, you just talk,
And make those awful squeaks upon the blackboard with your chalk.
You must make sure your shoes are wet and muddy,
And as for homework, you must guarantee you haven't studied.
You must put gum on everybody's seat,
And when there is a test you have to promise that you'll cheat.
Instead of teachers teaching you to make things,
The bad schoolteachers teach you how to break things:
They teach you how to smash a windowpane
And how to let a brand-new bike get rusty in the rain,
How to smash a vase to smithereens,
How to tear the pages out of someone's magazine,
How to hold your breath and spit and scream,
How to put mustard into someone's chocolate-chip ice cream,
How to bang a fender full of dents,
How to leave your footprint in a square of wet cement,
How to pinch and punch and slam a door,
How to splash water till you flood the bathroom floor,
How to do some muddy belly flops,
How to ruin your teeth with sugar pops,

How to turn a dress into a rag,
How to tear the bottom of a soggy garbage bag,
How to bend your father's fishing hook,
How to drip hot meatloaf gravy on your science book,
How to fill a bathtub up with glue,
How to bounce upon a bed until the springs pop through,
How to fall out of an apple tree,
How to scratch your toe and miss the toilet when you pee,
How to spread a coat of honey on a volleyball,
How to write your name in toothpaste on the bathroom wall,
How to snap a shoelace when you tie it—
These are all the things you'll learn
In nasty school—wanna try it?

For some schools you can't just be good—
You have to be the best.
Here you can't be rotten—
You must be the rottenest.

LESSON 7
HOW TO
BREAK
A VASE

WILD WEED

This kid-eating plant
Is a dangerous creature.
It can wind all around ya
And choke ya and eatcha.
I should chop it or clip it
Or pull it or prune it,
But its leaves are so pretty . . .
I *do* hate to ruin it.

FORGETFUL WITCH

I used to be a witching witch,
But now I'm just a watching witch
Watching other witches witching,
Wishing *I* could be bewitching.
But it's sad to tell
I can't recall one mystic curse
Or brew a poison. Even worse,
I cannot chant a deadly curse
Or cast a magic spell.
I can't turn princes into frogs
Or turn bad children into hogs.
I used to long ago, but now
I seem to have forgotten how.
Was it "Toads and snails and puppies' tails"?
Or "Toes and pails of guppies and whales"?
Or "Toast and bales of stale snail scales"?
I search my books and chew my nails
Wonderin' which is which,
'Cause a witch which can't bewitch
Just can't be a witch.

CRUNCH

I sat on the chair
And the chair just cracked.
I lay on the couch
And the whole thing snapped.
I tried out the swing
And it split six ways.
They're sure building furniture
Flimsy these days.

CLOUD WALKING

When you walk on clouds, be careful.
When you walk on clouds, beware,
And never look beneath your feet
To see what's under there.

LIAR, LIAR

"Liar, liar, your pants are on fire,
Your nose is as long as a telephone wire."
That's what they told me when I was a tot,
But now I am older,
My nose ain't no longer,
My pants ain't no hotter . . .
And I still lie a lot.

FOOD?

I was settin' at this restaurant
When the waiter came up and said, "What do you want?"
I looked at the menu—it looked so nice
Till he said, "Let me give you a little advice."
He said, "Spaghetti and potatoes got too much starch,
Pork chops and sausage are bad for your heart.
There's hormones in chicken and beef and veal,
Bowl of ravioli is a dead man's meal.
Bread's got preservatives, there's nitrites in ham,
Artificial coloring in jellies and jam.
Stay away from doughnuts, run away from pie,
Pepperoni pizza is a sure way to die.
Sugar's gonna rot your teeth and make you put on weight,
Artificial sweetener's got cyclamates.
Eggs are high cholesterol, too much fat in cheese,
Coffee ruins your kidneys and so do teas.
Fish got too much mercury, red meat is poison,
Salt's gonna send your blood pressure risin'.
Hot dogs and bologna got deadly red dyes,
Vegetables and fruits are sprayed with pesticides."
So I said, "What can I eat that's gonna make me last?"
He said, "A small drink of water in a sterilized glass."
And then he stopped and he thought for a minute,
And said, "Never mind the water—there's carcinogens in it."
So I got up from the table and walked out in the street,
Realizin' there was absolutely *nothing* I could eat.
So I haven't eaten for a month and I don't feel too fine,
But I know that I'll be healthy for a long, long time.

FRIEND

There's a bee on your head
Don't turn around
Don't move a muscle
Don't make a sound
Before he can sting you
I'll kill him dead
And you will be saved
From that bee on your head.

THE KID-EATING LAND SHARK

Said the shark down in the ocean,
"I do not understand
Why I'm starvin' in the water
When there's fresh kids on the land.
And why do folks keep sayin'
That a shark can't swim on shore
Just because no shark has ever
Tried it out before?"
So he swam up to the sandy shore
And burrowed with his fin,
And with a shout he stuck his snout
A centimeter in.
Another day—another inch,
Then two—then three—till he
Was swimmin' 'neath the land
The way he swam upon the sea.
Now he's prob'ly 'neath the sidewalk
While you run and jump and skate,
But you'll never ever see him—
Until it's much too late.
So let this be a lesson
To every shark and kid:
Just 'cause somethin' ain't been done
Don't mean it can't be did.
And when you're playing in your yard
You'd better get up fast
When you see a ziggin' zaggin' fin
Come zippin' through the grass.

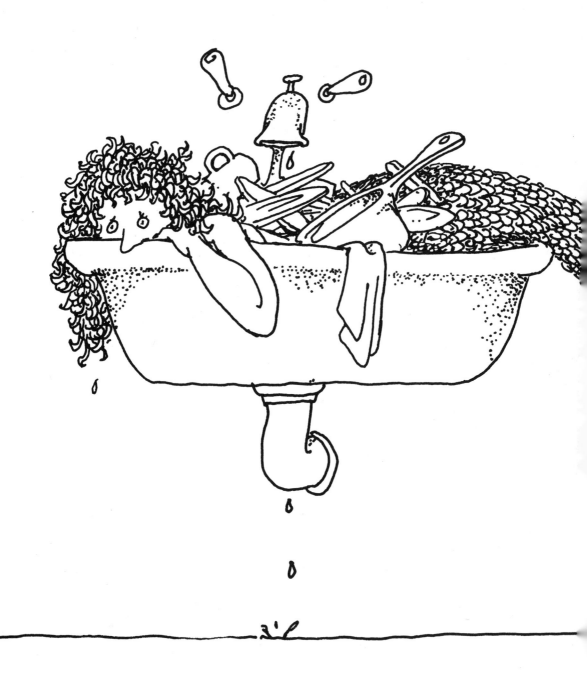

MER-MAID

We caught a mermaid in the creek.
We keep her in the sink.
We give her worms and snails to eat
And lemonade to drink.
She washes all the pots and pans.
She scrubs 'em with her scales.
She showers 'neath the faucet tap
And tells us fishy tales.
She sings us songs, she plays Go Fish,
She's happy as can be.
But now and then we catch her cryin',
Lookin' out to sea.

BETTY'S SPAGHETTI

Betty, Betty,
Sneezed in the spaghetti,
Made it icky and gooey and wetty.
So throw it out—it's ruined and lost,
Unless you like pasta
With sneezly sauce.

DIRTY FACE

Where did you get such a dirty face,
My darling dirty-faced child?

I got it from crawling along in the dirt
And biting two buttons off Jeremy's shirt.
I got it from chewing the roots of a rose
And digging for clams in the yard with my nose.
I got it from peeking into a dark cave
And painting myself like a Navajo brave.
I got it from playing with coal in the bin
And signing my name in cement with my chin.
I got it from rolling around on the rug
And giving the horrible dog a big hug.
I got it from finding a lost silver mine
And eating sweet blackberries right off the vine.
I got it from ice cream and wrestling and tears
And from having more fun than you've had in years.

GRUMBLING

Some people's stomachs gurgle and growl,
Some people's stomachs rumble and howl.
My stomach just begins to shout,
"No more ice cream and sauerkraut."

FOR A RAINY AFTERNOON

Nothing to do?
Nothing to do?
Pour some ketchup in your shoe.
Bang a drum and clang a bell,
Pinch the baby till he yells.
Spin around until you fall,
Draw a picture on the wall,
Put some marbles on the stair,
Stick some glue in Sister's hair.
Suck your thumb and slam the doors,
Pull out all the dresser drawers.
Catch the cat and bite his ear,
Soak your toes in Uncle's beer.
Fill your pockets full of soot,
Paint the bottom of your foot.
Take your grandpa's watch and boil it,
Throw the car keys down the toilet.
Wet your pants in Daddy's lap,
Now go upstairs and take your nap.

I DON'T KNOW

I don't know how *anything's* done.
Does the earth turn or is it the sun?
Is electricity made by a kite?
Are star twinkles just the reflection of light?
How thunder is made and how engines run—
I don't know how *anything's* done.

I don't know where *anyplace* is.
Is Baltimore next to Cadiz?
Is Maui in North or in South Carolina?
Do you pass Duluth on the highway to China?
I sure hope there isn't a test or a quiz
'Cause I don't know where *anyplace* is.

I don't know how *anything's* spelled.
Does lovely have three or four L's?
Don't you spell ewe with a Y or a U?
Does mulligatawny have one M or two?
It's time for exams and I'm not feeling well,
'Cause I don't know how *anything's* spelled.

I don't know who *anyone* was.
Was Charlemagne King Arthur's cuz?
Was Abraham Lincoln the prince of Tibet?
Was Nebuchadnezzar Queen Isabel's pet?
I sure hope they don't ask questions, because
I don't know who *anyone* was.

ELVINA

Poor Elvina, no one can find her.
They don't know she fell in the hamburger grinder.
They search through the salad,
They poke in the punch,
And none of them know
That they had her for lunch.

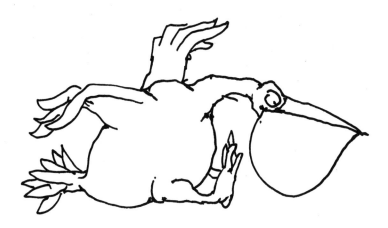

PELICAN EGG

I wanted to taste a pelican egg,
So I ran 'cross the ocean's sand,
Racin' and chasin' and almost tastin'
With my fryin' pan clutched in my hand.
Then I heard the flap of a feathered wing
And saw a pelican leg,
And plop! It fell right in my pan,
But it wasn't a pelican egg. . . .

KING TUT'S SKULL

This dusty skull was Ol' King Tut's.
I found it in this pyramid.
This tiny skull was King Tut's too
(From when he was a little kid).

THE PROBLEM

Jim copied the answer from Nancy
Sue copied the answer from Jim
Tim copied the answer from Sue, and then
Anne copied the answer from him
And Fran copied Anne and Jan copied Fran
The answer kept passing along
And no one got caught, but the problem was—
Nancy had it *wrong*.

BURPIN' BEN

Burpin' Ben, Burpin' Ben,
Learned to burp at the age of ten,
Thought it was funny and burped since then.
Anywhere and anywhen—
Burps at his parents, burps at his friends,
Burps at his sister, shy little Gwen;
Burps at his brother, poor little Len;
They say, "Gross," but he burps again.
Burps in the meadows, burps in the glen,
Burps at the robins, burps at the wrens.
They say, "Chirp," but he burps again.
Burps at the hogs in the farmer's pen,
Burps at the police and the firemen,
Burps in the Pledge of Allegiance, and when
They shout, "Halt," he burps again.
Burps at the teacher in school, and then
Burps on the bus goin' home again.
Burps in the zoo at the lion's den,
Burps in the movies, right at the end.
Burps in church when they say, "Amen."
They say, "Sin," but he burps again
And wonders why he hasn't a friend.
Hey—here he comes. "Well, hello, Ben."
"BURP"—there he goes again.

RASSLIN'

Rasslin' is a sweaty thing,
A rollin'-in-the-yard thing.
Tanglin' up's an easy thing,
Unrav'lin' is the hard thing.

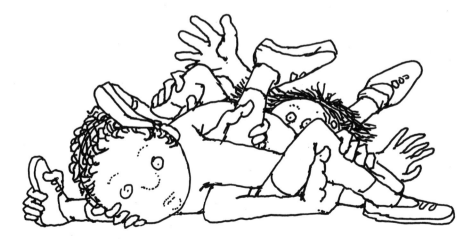

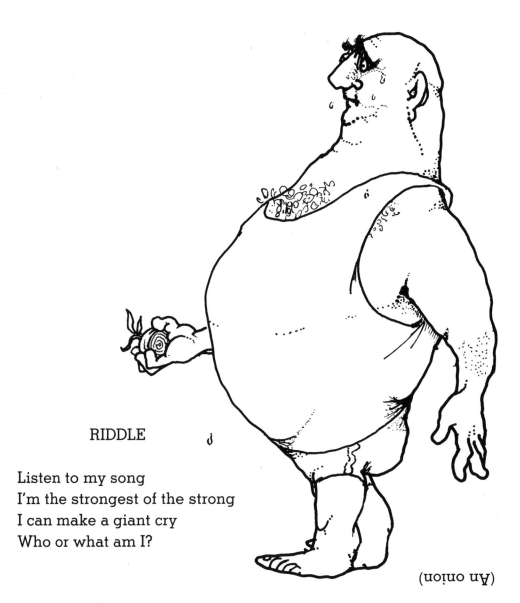

RIDDLE

Listen to my song
I'm the strongest of the strong
I can make a giant cry
Who or what am I?

(An onion)

EATIN' SOUP

Eatin' soup with chopsticks—
I should be finished soon.
Eatin' soup with chopsticks
While whistlin' a tune.
Eatin' soup with chopsticks
Because I have no spoon.
Eatin' soup with chopsticks
Can take all afternoon.

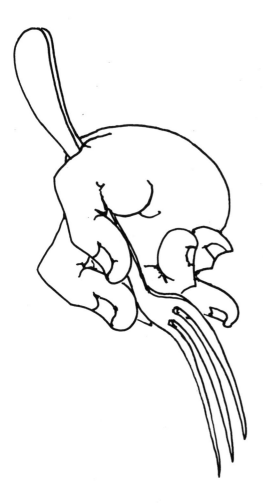

STORM

It's rainin' salt and pepper,
There's parsley comin' down,
Oregano falls just like snow
On everyone in town.

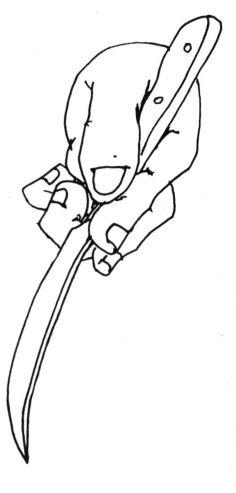

Look out—here comes some ketchup.
Now what's that in the sky?
A giant knife? A monstrous fork?
A napkin flapping high?
I think this is . . . good-bye.

JAKE SAYS . . .

Yes, I'm adopted.
My folks were not blessed
With me in the usual way.
But they *picked* me,
They *chose* me
From all the rest,
Which is lots more than most kids can say.

SMALL ZOO

The squeakin' mouse and the honkin' moose,
The nestin' grouse and the ganderin' goose,
The swingin' monkey and the spoutin' whale,
The kickin' donkey and the crawlin' snail,
The lumberin' ox and the hoppin' hare,
The sly ol' fox and the big brown bear,
The snappin' shark and the flyin' loon,
The singin' lark and the bold baboon,
The swimmin' sole and the great gorilla,
The diggin' mole and the armadillo,
The kangaroo and the nibblin' rat,
The cockatoo and the flappin' bat,
The porcupine and the polliwog,
The jungle lion and the croakin' frog,
The roarin' tiger and the deer . . .
Ain't here.

SPIDER

A spider lives inside my head
Who weaves a strange and wondrous web
Of silken threads and silver strings
To catch all sorts of flying things,
Like crumbs of thoughts and bits of smiles
And specks of dried-up tears,
And dust of dreams that catch and cling
For years and years and years. . . .

THE TOILET TROLL

Hi-ho for the toilet troll, troll, troll,
Down in the toilet bowl, bowl, bowl,
Slithering and scurgling
And slurming around
Under the water,
Not making a sound,
And waiting for you
To sit down,
　　　　　down,
　　　　　　　down.

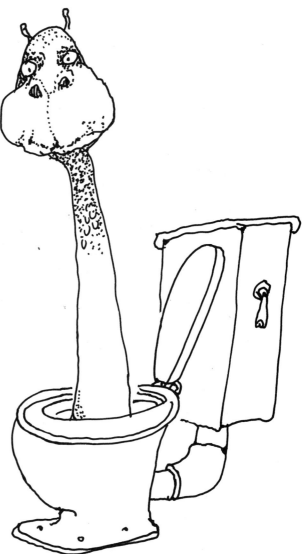

HAND LAND

Will you enter the land of the hands
Where fingers grow out of the sand?
Can you leave all your talk-listen language behind
And follow the signs?

WHEN I AM GONE

When I am gone what will you do?
Who will write and draw for you?
Someone smarter—someone new?
Someone better—maybe *YOU*!

INDEX

Our Thanks To:
Antonia Markiet, Jayne Carapezzi, Alyson Day,
Martha Rago, Rachel Zegar, Joy Kingsolver,
Catherine Hickey Hardin, David Billing, Edite Kroll, John Vitale,
Dorothy Pietrewicz, Lucille Schneider, Renée Cafiero.
And of course, to Susan Katz, Kate Morgan Jackson,
and the rest of the HarperCollins Children's Books team.

—The Family

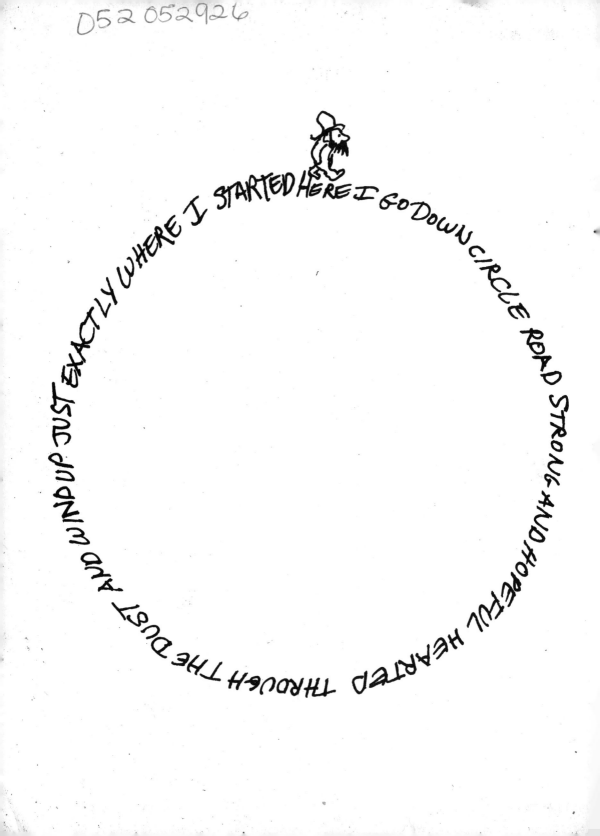

HERE I GO DOWN CIRCLE ROAD STRONG AND HOPEFUL HEARTED THROUGH THE DUST AND WIND UP JUST EXACTLY WHERE I STARTED